MEGA MAS

D1387388

Aliens v MAD Scientists
under the ocean

Nikalas Catlow
Tim Wesson

Draw your own adventure!

AIR CON

nosy crow

Mega Mash-Up: Aliens v Mad Scientists Under the Ocean

Published in the UK in 2011 by Nosy Crow Ltd
Crow's Nest, 11 The Chandlery
50 Westminster Bridge Road
London, SE1 7QY, UK

Registered office: 85 Vincent Square, London, SW1P 2PF, UK

Nosy Crow and associated logos are trademarks and or registered trademarks of Nosy Crow Ltd

Text and illustration copyright © Nikalas Catlow and Tim Wesson, 2011

The right of Nikalas Catlow and Tim Wesson to be identified as the authors and illustrators
of this work has been asserted by them.

A CIP catalogue record for this book is available from the British Library

ISBN: 978 0 85763 009 4

Your hand

This book needs

YOU!

What if the Earth was in terrible peril?

What if some **Mad Scientists** built

a machine UNDER THE OCEAN to save the day?

Would some pesky **ALiens** come along

and **zap** everything with their FRAZZELIZERS?

Would we all end up as **ALien Drones**?

You'll have to finish the illustrations
and find out...

Prepare to **LAUGH** while you doodle

and SNIGGER while you read.

Visit our awesome
website and get involved!
www.megamash-up.com
Upload artwork and get
the latest news

INTRODUCING the Aliens!

★ Snoogle-Busker ★

★ The Blob ★

★ Toot ★

★ Zarkov ★

★ Snaffloid ★

INTRODUCING the Mad Scientists!

★ Dr Nerdy ★

★ Dr Batty ★

★ Professor Egghead ★

★ Dr Crackers ★

★ Dr Daft ★

You'll need these...

DRAWING TOOLS

These are the **3** tools that Nikalas and Tim have used to create the artwork in this book.

PEN

crayon

felt-tip pen or marker

pencil

wax crayon

Using different tools helps create great drawings

texture page

pen zigzags

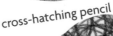

crayon rubbing from lino floor

cross-hatching pencil

crayon rubbing from floor

pencil rubbing from wooden door

scribbly pencil

There are loads of ways you can add texture to your artwork. Here are a few examples

crayon rubbing from wall

pencil dashes

DRAWING TIP!
Turn to the back of the book for ideas on stuff you might want to draw in this adventure

pen circles

Get Ready for a Really Sketchy adventure!

Pencils at the Ready...

On your marks...

Let's Draw!

Chapter 1

Keep the Earth Spinning!

A **Mad Scientist** is on the phone to the President.
"Professor Egghead here. We have a problem.
In 48 hours, the Earth will stop spinning and everything
on it will float away! We think those pesky
Aliens are at it again, Sir..."

Inside a nearby Alien spaceship, three Aliens are congratulating themselves. "Ha! Ha! Our ingenious **FrictionRAY**™ is working!" cackles Zarkov. "Soon the Earth will be ours!"

What are they watching on the Alien eye?

Create a vapourizer dial

Add more Alien symbols

"We have a plan, Mr President, Sir!" cries Professor Egghead. "We will build the **Mighty Magnetizer** under the Ocean and keep the World turning!"
"Get on with it, then!" snaps the President. "Time is running out..."

Finish inventing the Mighty Magnetizer

What does a titanium water turbine look like?

Draw a defence outpost on the ocean bed

But an Alien called Snoogle-Busker has been listening in. "Action stations!" he bellows into his wrist-com. "**Attack! Attack!** The Scientists are building a machine to save the Earth! DESTROY THEM!"

Add another Alien horn

Create strange Alien listening devices

Meanwhile, back under the Ocean, the Scientists have hit a **CRUSTY PROBLEM**. "Barnacle build-up on the outer ring," Dr Crackers informs Base. "Send out the **BARNACLE BUSTER!**"

Show the Reactor you designed in more detail!

Who is in the window?

Finish the seabed

"Ooh, it's scary out here," whimpers Dr Loopy.
"Who knows what's **LURKING IN THE DARK**?"

What else is lurking in the murky depths?

What's in the creepy cave?

Add more bubbling geysers to the seabed

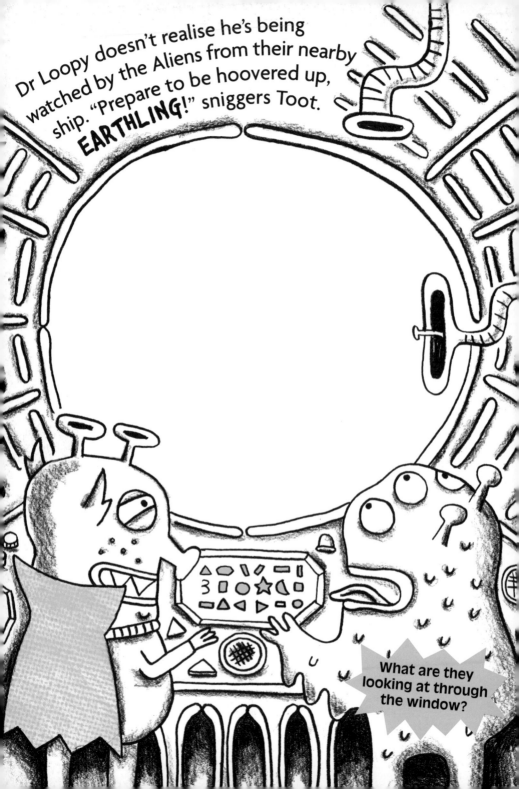

Chapter 2
Alien Antics

"Left a bit!" shouts Toot. "I mean, right a bit!"
"HMMZZ FRUUURRP!" mutters the
Blob, yanking the gearstick
around crossly, before sucking up
the **BARNACLE BUSTER**.
"Got it!"
cries Toot.

Add another Alien vessel

I've not seen that before

What else is getting sucked into the ship?

Meanwhile, Zarkov and Snaffloid have smashed through an airlock and are making a grab for Dr Crackers. "Mind you **DON't PULL HiS HEaD OFF!**" laughs Zarkov.

This is the radio room. Is everything all right down there?

What is Dr Crackers spluttering here?

What is pouring in with the sea water?

HULL BREACH SEAL DOORS

But Radio Mike has witnessed the attack and raises the alarm.

"Aliens! Gone! Crackers!"

"**FERP-BURM-EEERT-LAAARG!**" laughs the Blob.
"Great idea, Blobby – let's turn them into Alien Drones!"

The Blob's got a list of nasty jobs for the Drones . . .

Radio Mike barges into the Mad Scientists' **CHILLAX-ZONE**. "Didn't you hear the alarm? The Aliens are attacking and the **Magnetizer** isn't working yet – we're DOOMED!"

What virtual game are they playing?

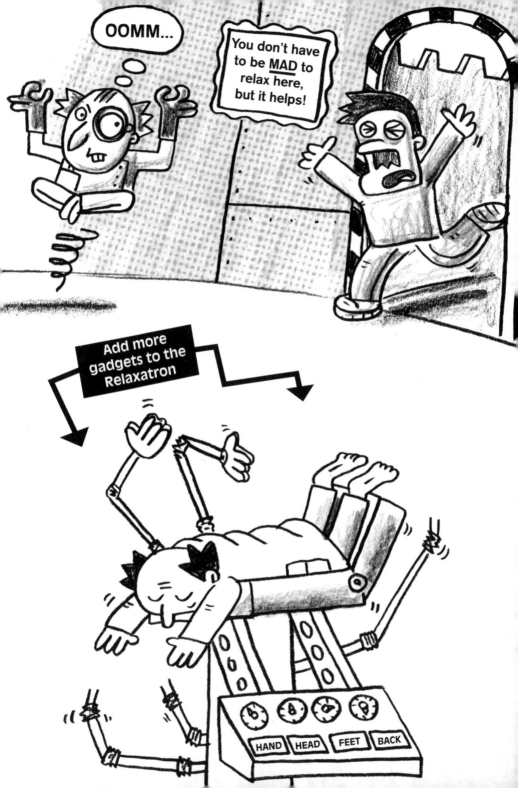

Suddenly,
Egghead gets a call.
"Scientists!" barks the President.
"Is the **MAGNETIZER** complete yet?"
"Er, not quite," stammers the Professor.
"There's been a slight
technical hitch . . ."

Is the President angry or worried?

Egghead

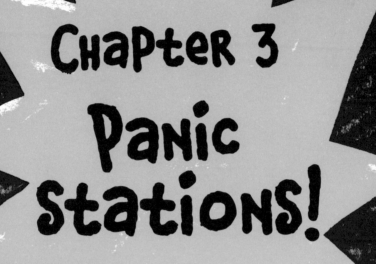

Chapter 3
Panic stations!

"Launch Alien attack-vessels," orders Zarkov. "Last Alien to board the **Magnetizer** smells of fish," laughs Snoogle-Busker. "**Oi!**" complains a passing **Cod.**

Finish Snaffloid and Snoogle-Busker's pod

What's on the end of this arm?

Finish the seabed

Release the terrifying Squidzilla

Professor Pickle-Brain releases his latest monstrous creation – **Squidzilla**. "Go get 'em, my beauty," he murmurs. Dr Nerdy activates his pump-action Piranha Cannons. "I have Aliens in my sights!" he cries. **PAH! PAH! PAH! PAH! PAH!** go the Piranha Cannons.

Engage the pump-action Piranha Cannons!

"What are these weird creatures?" asks Zarkov. "Are they genetically modified? That'll never do!" **ZAPPPPP!!!**

But a piranha has got into the ship's steering device and Zarkov has **LOST CONTROL**. "Watch out for that spinny thing!" shrieks Snoogle-Busker. "**EJect! EJect!**"

Show the wreckage from an Alien pod crashing into a turbine and exploding!

Oooh! That's nasty

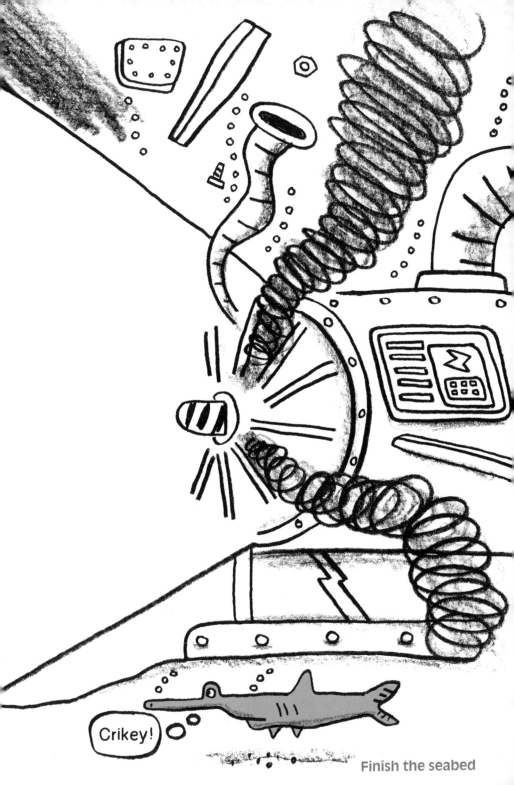

Finish the seabed

Chapter 4
Alien Drones

The Aliens re-group and **BASH, MASH** and **SMASH** their way into the **MIGHTY MAGNETIZER!**

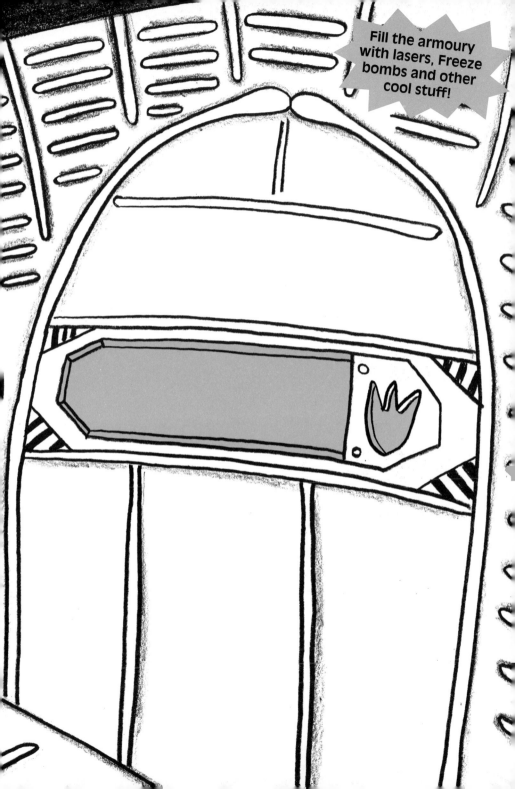

Finish Toot's frazzle frenzy!

Dr Nerdy and Professor Egghead are the first to be Droned. "Not bad," laughs Zarkov. "But maybe **tweak** the setting a bit."

This Mad Scientist looks scared

The Mad Scientists are shocked!

"Right, you can start by washing my pants, Drones," says Toot, pointing to a **Steaming** pile in the corner.

Chapter 5
What a Daft Idea!

Meanwhile in G-lab, Dr Daft has come up with a plan. **"WE'LL DISGUISE OURSELVES AS ALIENS** and rescue the other Mad Scientists! Put that on, Batty, but don't forget to cut eye-holes!"

Add lab equipment here

Draw everything that Batty needs for his Alien disguise

Add strange sea
creatures here

Add more engine parts

Cover the engine room in oozing Alien goo!

The two Mad Scientists follow Alien goo to the engine room. "We're getting close," whispers Dr Batty. "There's gloop everywhere. Pull your **SQUID** down, Daft, we're going in!"

What does Dr Batty look like in disguise?

Zarkov is so busy **DRONING** on he doesn't notice Daft and Batty peeping round the door, wearing their suspect Alien disguises.

What Drone-like sounds are they making?

But then...
"OH NO!" exclaims Dr Batty. "**My disguise is snagged**!"
"Intruders!" screeches Zarkov. "Stop them!"

Finish the control panel

RiiiP!

"SPPPPOOOODDLE POOOPT!" slurps the Blob,
morphing towards the hapless Scientists.
"RUN FOR IT!" shrieks Dr Daft.

CONTROL ROOM

Finish the chase scene all the way to the control room!

"**So long, losers**," puffs Dr Batty. "Quick, Daft! To the control room. It's time for plan Batty!"

Sealing themselves into the control room,
Dr Batty gets to work. "I can **OVERRIDE the
DRONE-CONVERTING** machine from here,
but it won't be easy . . ."

Yikes! What's
bothering Dr Daft?

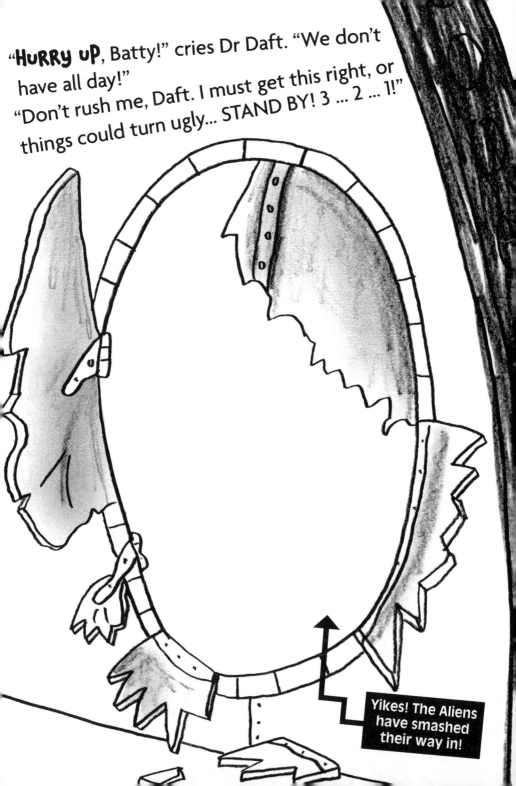

"**HURRY UP**, Batty!" cries Dr Daft. "We don't have all day!"

"Don't rush me, Daft. I must get this right, or things could turn ugly... STAND BY! 3 ... 2 ... 1!"

Yikes! The Aliens have smashed their way in!

"Uh-oh," says Dr Daft. "I know you said things could turn ugly, but this is **RIDICULOUS!**"

Chapter 6

The Blob's a Genius!

It's a real mix-up! Everyone is half-Alien, half-Scientist.

"**THiS iS SO COOL**!" laughs Pickle-Brain.
"I really love my new hair!" says Zarkov.

What does Zarkov look like?

Pickle-Brain

Oh my! I seem to be making perfect sense!

Finish Toot's transformation

Add another genetic mix-up

"That's funny," says Crackers.
"My glasses are lifting off!"
"Oh no!" remembers Pickle-Brain. "We're losing gravity. **THE END OF THE WORLD IS NIGH!**"

"**Excuse me, Gentlemen**," says the Blob. "I believe I have the answer..."

Uh-oh! What else is floating away?

"You simply need to **REBALANCE THE QUANTUM FLUX** on the **MAGNETIZER** BEFORE turning the ignition," he says, cleverly.

"You did it!" cries the President.
"You must all have a **Nobel Prize**. But what's happened to your nose, Egghead?"
    "Oh, just a small side effect of saving the world, Mr President, Sir!"

Finish the pile up as everyone hits the ground

What an AMAZING week it's been under the Ocean.
The Mad Scientists built a **Magnetizer**. The Aliens tried
to **destroy it!**

They all **ZAPPED** each other, then together they stopped the Earth from grinding to a halt. **HURRAH!**

Picture Glossary

If you get stuck or need ideas, then use these pages for reference.

Alien Pod

Scientists' Communication Gadgets

Alien Listening Device

Explosion

If you like, you can copy the pictures. OR you can draw your own version.

Sea Creatures

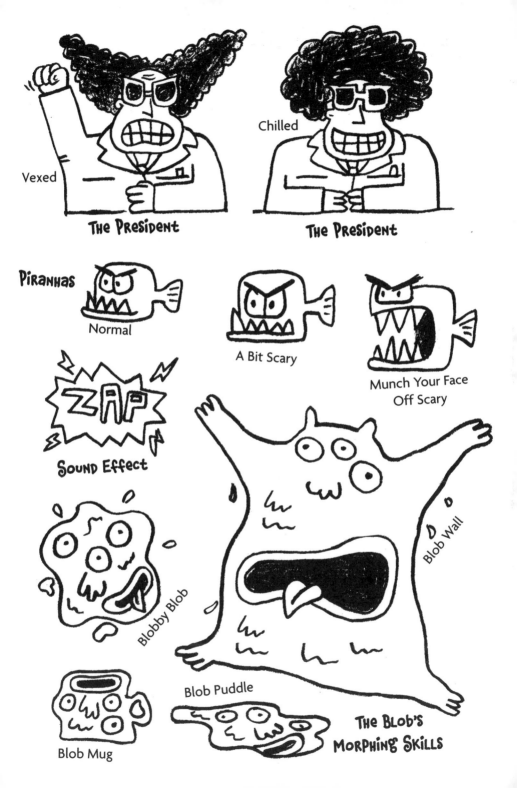

Picture Glossary

If you get stuck or need ideas, then use these pages for reference.

Alien Expressions

Laughing

Cunning

Really Mad

Tim's Squidzilla

Nikalas' Squidzilla

If you like, you can copy the pictures. OR you can draw your own version.

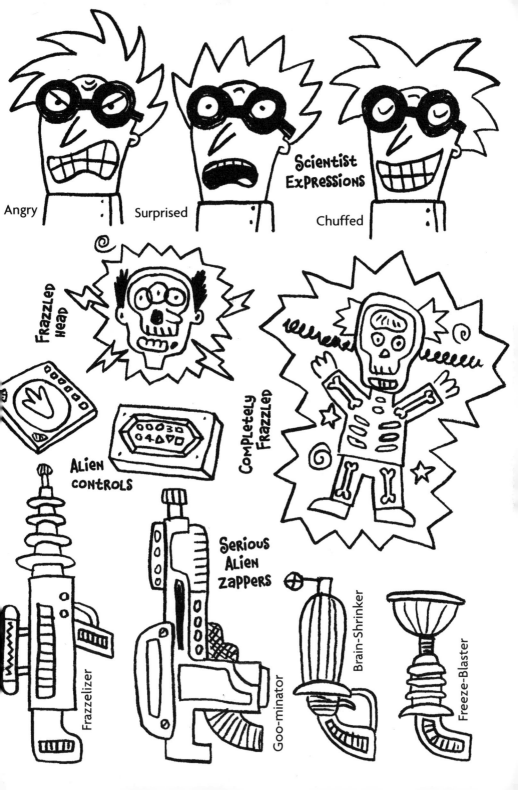

Scientist Expressions

Angry

Surprised

Chuffed

Frazzled Head

Completely Frazzled

Alien Controls

Serious Alien Zappers

Frazzelizer

Goo-minator

Brain-Shrinker

Freeze-Blaster